An Anthology of

The Heart, Mind, and Spirit

By

K. Renee

Foreword:

Some say our souls whisper to us our true desires and to be happy all we as humans have to do is listen.

Contents

Sophic Circumspection

This section is dedicated to the heart. Thoughts on possible occurrences that will affect an individual's emotions; such as love, fear, anger, etc...

1406 Bedroom Theme	Nothing Compares to
your Choco lateness	
Cheater	Off the Dome
Cinnamon	Parental Caution
Common Interest	Serious Thoughts
Face it	Sincerity within
Diversity	
Head Games	So Sick
Inevitably Connected	Ten Years and Still in Love
Love – 2010 Style	Truthfully

Cognitive Disturbance

This section is dedicated to the mind. Thoughts on possible occurrences that will affect an individual mentally with many of the twists and turns life sends one's way; such as betrayal, manipulation, and the games people play.

A Man's World	Feigning
Banging Personalities	Hotness
Can you Hear me now	Listen to your Own Self
Cohabitation	Name Calling
Emotional Today	The ATES that ACHE
Excited over Nothing	Up Tow

Numinous Sapience

This section is dedicated to the spirit. Thoughts on possible occurrences that will affect an individual's spirit – to hopefully provide hope and encouragement when one feels downtrodden.

    Advice   Inspired by Friendship

    At any Cost   Lessons and Blessings

    Butterflies   My Heart Don't Pump no Slushy

    Can't U See   Read in the Sky

    Domestic Violence   Sympathy

    Empathy   Think Before You Speak

    I can see through your mask   Too Much of Anything

    Why Some Black Women Mean Mug

Orphic Astuteness

This section is dedicated to profound imagery. As we are all just humans on this journey called life, this chapter is a pool, in which is gathered the ramblings of the author of this work.

After Work	Rationale
Cupcakes	Satisfied but
Still Hungary	
Dropped from Heaven	Sexual
Orientation	
Fruity Fantasies	Shadows in Smoke
Grown Folk Passion	Spontaneity

Muse   Trippin'
                                  Why I Write

HEART

1406 Bedroom Theme…

The theme of this here is genuinely exquisite

Although at times I shy away from what it takes to exhibit

The texture and dexterity required to make this pairing work

Last night was enough to cause a kneejerk

By that I mean a simultaneous reaction

No one compares to you in the bedroom faction

The act of letting go and handing over to me your constitution

Your moans and exclamations drive me to be wanton with abandon...

Hedge me on...to keep going, and going...

With your head thrown back and legs spread - the center of you showing...

Anxious and intoxicated by the scent of you.

Even more so as that session was just a preview...

To what I want - no need from your end in a few days...

My turn to moan - and scream out your name.

Cheater

I can still smell you on my clothes

You were holding me so close

Your arms around me felt delicious always anxiously awaiting another dose.

Being in your presence leaves me in a daze

From the top of your head to the bottom of your feet - amazed.

It's a secret whenever we meet – this passion is rationed because we must be discreet.

I was trying to be faithful – a good girl you see.

But just talking to you – I knew what it would be...

It started not too long ago

I would see you going about your business to and fro

One day our eyes met, we smiled, sat and had a conversation – clever

Soon we were talking on the phone – interesting - could talk to you forever

When I lay my head down at night you are my last thought

And when I wake – I see your face – be careful bout to mess around and get caught

I was trying to be faithful – a good girl you see.

But just talking to you – I knew what it would be...

Honestly feeling as if I'm the first person to feel heat at this degree.

The most erotic thing about you is you see the real me...

Your stare is so intense – with those gorgeous deep brown eyes

One glance alone makes heat creeps up my thighs

All it takes is a brush of our skin – yes the slightest touch

It makes me tingle all over – it's just too much.

I was trying to be faithful – a good girl you see

But just talking to you – I knew what it would be…this passion - it's the only reason I would cheat.

Cinnamon is a Spice Only

Dove head first into irises the color of cinnamon

A glimpse of a flicker of fire caught my attention…

Such a romantic – eager to be warmed in your heat

Initially that was my only intention…

Neglected to notice a tendency toward coldness in your eyes

Even ignored that habit you have toward not listening when loving – it's something you exhibit fully without any disguise

Naive of me to be convinced I possess the tool to unlock the passion you so carefully hold in check

I've said and done too much to be
granted that key I suspect...

Common Interest

You always understand what I am saying..

Can even distinguish that slight nuance of when I am serious or playing…

I love the rhythm in which you move

Neither fast nor slow - just right at your own groove…

Your smile chases away any worry I may have

No matter -to see your face I am always glad…

My attraction to you is not purely sexual

The most arousing part of me you reach stems from the intellectual…

It's hard to explain as I'm feeling you in so many ways

It's obvious yet so apprehensive about how to display…

Face it - It's Over

Why are we still here…do we stay in something so unfulfilling out of fear?

…you don't understand me or I you…our daily routines vary – neither identifying with what the other is going thru.

Thoughts of you yield so many feelings all resulting in confusion, when I attempt to express this to you it only contributes to this delusion - of bonding, happiness, and love - this back and forth…it may sound arrogant but I feel somehow above.

We are individuals who are cut from two different types of cloth - unalike in so many ways but in regard to each other soft.

Like putty – where every unkind word leaves a bruise - never finding the source of this ill contempt only results in the feeling of being manipulated and misused.

Well at least for me anyway - When I look into your eyes only emptiness shows and the beginning of the need to stray.

Perhaps your irises are only acting as the clearest mirror…my heart tells me something within is making you feel inferior.

So much potential existed in our initial pairing, daring to be a part of one another's lives - living and sharing…

But like many relationships - we were so optimistic - no plans did we make…

absolutely no preparations for this earthquake.

This silence and lack of common interest has shaken us to our core···the reason each of us is still here is because we are both so unsure.

Where will we go···who will know me as I know you and vice versa. Falling in love should come with a disclaimer -do not attempt this without several years of rehearsal.

I reluctantly admit I am afraid to step out on that ledge - insecure about what is around that lonely corner – yes it makes me hedge···

But it cannot be any worse than what is going on now···getting closer to home should never cause a frown to appear upon one's brow.

But it does - daily···with increasing frequency. But how do I cut this umbilical cord - this dependency.

A wise person advised - just walk out - don't look back···get in the first thing smoking and go···I could never do this but the more I think about it my anticipation of leaving you grows.

Just visualizing being in my own space again makes me downright giddy. I can come and go as I please or purchase any item without the consult of a damn committee…

It is really a pity that we are still here - no two people should remain in a relationship out of fear.

Head Games

I can feel it when you come into a room…

All the air is sucked out - how I imagine it would feel inside a vacuum.

Only there is no whooshing sound - only your voice…

You're the selected item; with headphones …ignoring you is not a choice.

The phrases you utter are music to my ears…

Giving a false sense of security - systematically - making me believe there is nothing to fear.

Feeling me with warmth and making my imagination come to life…

What would be your reaction if you knew my desire for you at night?

Fantasizing about how you would be with all those layers you are wrapped in pulled away…

Sprawled naked before me with no pressing engagements to melee.

I can feel it when you step into any room…

Your scent alone gives it away - causing mental stimulation - and the urge to consume.

Devour - yes, even be greedy and dominate all of your time…

Secretly jealous if any other has the attention of what I' ve convinced myself is all mine.

Inevitably Connected

What is the connection between us two?

It hypnotizes, dizzying and stirring... albeit I don't believe in voodoo...
The only explanation – it must be love.
Opposites yet - fitting snug as a glove...

It has been years since I first saw your face.
Devoted, loyal, and true – you I would never disgrace...
It was slow going to get you to fully commit.
But now your devotion you rush to remit...

This is just a little note to let you know.
I appreciate the way you nurture making sure our union grows...
In your arms I feel warmth and content.
You are the perfect package for me – grateful daily that you were sent...

Love - 2010 Style

How in the hell?

You say you love me…yet are afraid to share or even tell

As if - if I knew the real – your demise I would rush to excel…

Concealing truths out of fear of coming out of that vigilant shell

So convinced if I know …I am a sort of super being who will cast you under my spell…

I love you so I ask myself those types of questions - as yearning for your understanding is where I dwell

Chemistry and intellect like no other only a few reasons my cheek is consistently on your lapel

Therefore making this battle called us only for hours at a time quell…

How in the hell?

Your hesitancy is just pushing this one to say farewell…

Cringing each time you ring my phone or oh no…not the doorbell…

But the physical - those maneuvers - the clarity in your eyes makes me hold tight looking forward to the next impel…

You're the actions speak louder than words type always sure to make not just my heart swell⋯

But I am saying though ⋯ how in the hell?

Albeit I have several eager for the chance to just once be allowed to pamper this bombshell⋯

It's futile to even bother with that as yours is the only soul in which I gel⋯

What am I to do about this dilemma that upon my lap has befell?

All I can do is shake my head and wonder how in the hell⋯

Nothing Compares to Your Chocó lateness

Fantasizing all day about your chocolate skin until I am about to swoon

So much so – got me contemplating attacking you this afternoon

Every fiber of my being needs you to act real soon

As I am ready for you to take me to the moon...

Like you've got a rocket in your pocket made just for me

Before takeoff you know how to get me to the right degree

The feel of your hands and mouth in all the right spots

Anxiously awaiting your next onslaught...

When you take me this time — there is no required gentleness

By this I mean no need to treat me like an empress.

Just bring that passion you are so good at...

That thunder...that truth — my chocolate wildcat.

Off the Dome

Heartache is a lonely and desolate state.

Without a doubt or the slightest hint of room to debate

But is a realm in which I would rather dwell — than your presence — as of late

Yet again - I will attempt to express myself - just so you can get this straight

Your lack of ability to understand me is the main vein of this heartbreak.

Hello - is anyone home - damn – were you always this slow to relate?

I don't mind being the stronger of us two (sometimes) – but I MUST always feel – I can count on my teammate

No more of your weak excuses - is my new mandate…

You just had too many – so this thing called us - I had to abate

Felt more like I had two kids instead of one – and was carrying deadweight.

Hello - is anyone home - damn, are you serious… were you always this slow to relate?

Now who's to say when – or if I will find another – as an appropriate bedmate?

At least when I put my head to pillow I won't feel stressed or anything that frustrates

So irritated by you in my heart and mind – there has been the release of a floodgate

Of my ability to protect myself - win this competitive game of wills and scream checkmate!

Got me protecting my own neck – convinced it only matters if – I and one other – have ate…

Hello - is anyone home - are you serious… were you always this slow to relate?

More regrets – than hopeful thoughts – are what seal the deal – in us no longer being mates

I see you clearly now – as if a visit to the doctor has caused my eyes to dilate

You're afraid to be the man you could be – and would rather hold – the title of lightweight

It's finally done – with no more room to placate.

Damn – why didn't I see sooner - you were so slow to relate?

Parental Caution

See at 21 - I was turned out.

Not by a stranger running some game - but surprisingly by the one from whose womb I sprout.

It is hard for some to even believe.

But this is real talk people - coming from the heart - too painful a thing for pretend or un-useful as a tool to deceive.

Everyone is not meant to be a mother.

Catch the wrong one - as soon as it's realized - run for cover…

Serious Thoughts

I'm in love with you

Doing everything possible…

To keep you from seeing thru

My facade…it's so hard, this job - this task, hiding behind a mask

Because your presence is the most exhilarating essence

But a confession - any admission - on any condition - could end - this trend…

Of smiling and joking with my friend

In my dreams - the theme…would be no schemes

Only sunlight – that delight, deep insight and communication

No doubt – that mental fornication

I'm in love with you

Doing everything possible…

To keep you from seeing thru

What you do to me…it's the truth.

So funny - no dummy - an intellectual in fact

Can get an attitude - be rude - but with eyes so deep

One who looks and seeks can see that soul won't creep…

If anyone is listening…this one is complete.

I'm in love with you

Do you have a clue?

Am I keeping you from seeing thru?

My ambush…and facade, it's so hard, this job - this task, hiding behind this damned mask

You're the truth…I'm in love with you…

Sincerity within Diversity

I love you - for so many reasons.

These feelings go on and on thru any season...

You can make me smile or cause me to frown.

There is no telling which when you are around...

No matter where I go you are in my thoughts.

To be in your good graces is the only item sought...

Deep within your heart are so many precious jewels.

Wrapped in layers of defense - to remove takes special tools...

These special devices only I possess.

To cause certain concessions and the pardons you profess...

These feelings go on and on thru any season.

I love you - for so many reasons...

So Sick

I am feeling sad and blue... You don't know what I am going through

It's only been one day, since you've been away

My heart is lonely for you…I don't know what to do…

I sit around looking at the door…wondering if I would see you any more

Long for your touch and kiss…if only you were here to help with this

Missing your laugh and that sexy smile…being without you is like a new lifestyle

I love the way that you make me feel…the chemistry between us is so real

So sick, this feeling I can't explain…. These feelings are so hard to maintain

I can't eat, I can't sleep… without you in my life I can't go on

Ten Years and Still In Love…

The moment I laid eyes on you - I knew you would have an effect on me in some way

My intuition is sharp, it turned out to be true but your effect was uncanny…

The vibe I get from you is so amazing and full of electricity

You are three dimensional – always supplying some form of duplicity…

Never meaning to throw shade in the way you talk and deal

Unabashedly open and in the same instance hesitant to reveal...

Your character is intriguing but sometimes makes me afraid

Of what will happen in testy situations when a choice has to be made...

The variables in our equation always make me feel unsure

Is this commitment for life or just something for right now to make us each feel secure...?

Questions like these swirl around my mind sometimes

And then I am in your arms again confident everything will be just fine...

Whatever lies beyond the horizon in any regard to us

You will always be the greatest love of my life, this is a fact - do trust.

Truthfully

I am all yours truthfully...

Our bond is strong mentally and physically.

Unbreakable by disagreement – or anything petty and silly...

So grateful to have you – really...

Before I rest at night you must be lying beside me.

If you are anywhere else rest skips our bedroom completely...

In the morning when I wake your face I must see.

This is never up for debate and you always comply faithfully...

Some may doubt this relationship of ours.

Wondering why these two dimes connection has not soured...

But to all the haters I simply say.

This here closeness will outlast yours any day...

MIND

This is a man's World

Mama always warned – it is a cold cruel world

This is so true – especially if one happens to be born a girl…

You have to be tough yet soft in this wilderness called life

Too slow or too quick – brings on constant items of strife…

Remain in the middle for balance and the ability to cope despite

Challenges, emotional impulses and everyday occurrences that just ain't right…

Always make your own choices and ignore attempts at pushing into situations

Even those who are considered true friends – if unsure-only look heavenward for inspiration…

Banging Personalities

    Some folk have a glow – you know

    This light, so bright, it can be
    frightening – blinding because it shines
    as if you are looking into the sun

    Being around them is so much fun –
    making even those as wide as all
    outside want to break out and run

Can you Hear me now?

When certain energies combine powerful things can occur

This bond can be precarious and requires attention so it won't sour…

Intuition will always register parting after a disagreement is undesirable

As each contributes equal amounts any damage after any spat is only minimal…

Respect for one another in a pairing is essential to happiness

It's the truth – bringing the purest of emotion – but most important trustworthiness…

These things and more are what I hope – yes even know we have the potential to share

I pray for strength and fortitude to show you how much I care…

When I look into your eyes I am always taken back by the decency resonating within you

My perception is clear that you will hold steady no matter what we go thru…

And I will too…

No matter what you do…

I know you're not that into words but no worries my actions will prove I am telling the truth

When we touch I am filled with the strongest of sensations…

The most dizzying being that your bedroom is not our exclusive destination

Cohabitating

You are what I need, want and desire

Creative in your approach at sparking, reinforcing and sustaining this fire…

That you all alone created within my soul

My well –being is only maintained as it is definite by twilight you I will hold…

By sunset with the rising of the moon I look toward the sky tingling with anticipation

Knowing soon we will be behind our door alone makes our address my beloved destination…

Emotional Today

Throat feels tight as if in it something is stuck

Afraid to swallow this knot as a tear may fall – all choked up

Thinking of what must be done to escape the emptiness of being your woman

Was resolved and composed until hearing a tune – now emotions are consuming

All the things we've shared over the years are running thru my mind

Progressions along with cohesive intimacy are the two main lines we did not find…

In regard to you – I have finally reached the end of my rope

Your well-being and happiness are no longer priorities into which energy I devote

See – our tussle has made me acutely aware of what I need in a mate…

A God fearing, intelligent, strong yet gentle king is a must have – on this I will no longer settle or debate

Your habits have not and will not change no matter how I plead or attempt to help

The only thing left to do is remove my things and myself…

Annoyed at the tune that drifted into my hearing zone early this morn

Certain verses had been avoided – no radio for me as those sappy loves songs have been shorn…

The words I had been dreading drifted from my own musical collection

The melody, words and familiar rhythm brought on the deepest retrospection…

Nostalgic visions of how we used to be - should be - and could be flooded my senses

Angered as could have, should have, and would have is a backward course – taken by only the simplest and densest…

Which I am not one of…or am I…okay I admit I was for you

This is the kind of thing I detest going thru

Failed again at love should be tattooed across my skin

I am hurt, disgusted, and sore but not apprehensive about trying again…

I will continue on my journey of life - just not with you

It is sad but a fact I must face and do what I have to do…

Excited Over Nothin'

> Revved up as if I am the sleekest ride
> ever seen by any whose gaze crosses
> my path…

Every step – enticing – flesh glistening as I have just stepped out of my bath…

Ready to give you every inch of me – yes- open myself all the way…

The trust you granted revealing your vulnerabilities had a melting effect on me today…

Dissolving all my defenses such heavy garments I always carry with me…

As I lay back, staring into your eyes…excited to be finally sharing completely…

Each kiss and caress makes me cry out – aching but not in agony…

Even whisper my desires in your ear which you oblige amply…

Covered in sweat from scalp to toe…

Grasping each other tightly convinced neither wants to let go…

Just as I have sucked oxygen into my lungs for the most content of exhales…

Your grip loosens and you let go - causing our heat and passion to derail…

Before you place your feet on the floor I whimper to let you know to stay put…

Going so far as to lean into you to exemplify my hunger is not kaput…

This goes unnoticed as you stand beginning to busy yourself about…

I silently stare as this instant retreat has filled me with doubt…

Questioning our connection I stand pretending to busy myself too...

As you leave the room I am left to my own faculties of figuring out what to do...

Lie back down, wait, or clean myself up and leave...

As this room once so warm is now filled with the coolest breeze...

I choose the latter...once you notice you inquire of my need to go...

Playing it cool I mutter some excuse...annoyed that you do not already know...

Feigning

Feigning – there is something about you that lacks majesty... When I am in your presence – I witness this catastrophe...

Could it be the faḍade that enables me?

While watching you grasp for your destiny...

The touch from your hand is like an emotionless igloo... The friendship between us is slowing descending – who knew...

Feigning – for a piece of life that is no longer there! The aloofness in your eyes seems as if you don't care...

Anticipating the day you oust and divulge that the drama has passed...How previously emotions

scampered through your thoughts —
today does not last…

Seize those demons that deluge deceit into your heart… Cast away that animosity that compels reality apart…

Feigning – make believe, fake, and even pretend…I hope all this counterfeit behavior will soon end…

Hotness

Imitation is the purest form of flattery
Gives away a lack of originality to me…
Be who you are and if you don't know
Take the time to learn or within you won't grow…

> *Walking around trying to mimic my style because you have no clue*
> *You'd be more successful if you just be you*
> *Initiate to investigate what it takes to stand firm*
> *If being you is a test - you are failing this term*

Now I appreciate that you like what you see
Annoyed at your obtuse attitude of how I came to be
Nothing I can do or say would make you understand
Some of the difficulties overcome to get to where I am…

> *I know that this is frustrating no need to blame*
> *Just take a little time out and try to explain*
> *I want to know how you got to where you are*
> *Honestly, was the path you aimed for real far?*

Yielding this information is difficult for me
I will attempt to give you the real minus any hyperbole
It was a treacherous journey to wind up here
Unsure if any explanation will ever come across clear
Hurdles in the past and some even today

You have to be agile – up for any required role that needs to be played…

I empathize - that you want to keep your past secrets within

However, that is not telling me how this path of your life begin

We all ascended hills, and submerged obstacles like a hurricane whirlwind

Excoriate a layer one at a time until your images revealed becomes paper thin

Confide in me as if we shared the same womb – minds and souls as one – connected my twin

Confidence is something I usually hesitate to yield

Wrapping myself in layers placing indifference on my face as a shield

My path has been challenging but no more than any others

When putting my head to pillow I rest – no hint of nightmare to make me shudder

If you can muster the strength and character it takes to be a true friend

I welcome the connection of a twin on whom to depend

Looking forward to this unison forged by two women of color

As we possess gifts that go untapped in any other…

Assurance is something you possess deep down inside

Take a moment; look in the mirror there is nothing to hide

See you can understand the roads are rocky like many others

Go ahead express yourself – write, dance or even if just utter

I know the meaning of a true friend; I am one - Yes indeed!

Trust, honesty and loyalty – just believe in me & take heed…

The connection is strong like a bond between a child & their mother

I agree! The forces between two beautiful intelligent women of color
- no wonder…

I struggle with the messages I attempt to convey

So sensitive and easily overwhelmed at times it creates a melee

A breach in my ability to feel the pulse of this thing called life

As it is a necessity to plug in and perform despite

My energy level or the desire to just create and chill

This machine – our society takes over as if it breathes and has its own will

But with persistence and the determination to see this thing thru

I got you on this – no doubt this combined force is the truth…

> *There are trials and tribulations that may cause you exertion*
> *Being cognizant is part of maturing and learning life's lesson*
> *What is the aperture that makes you feel so timid?*
> *I know some people around may cause you to become livid*
> *You have to take the good with the bad and don't get amiss*
> *Move those haters around to prove you got this…*

Here is an attempt to state clearly why I am this way

Disrespect, deceit and death are the three items that almost led me astray

To save my soul I had to become apt at burying myself and create a way to portray

A persona that can blend into this illusion dealt with day by day…

> *I'm ecstatic you decided to reveal why there's so much distance*
> *The 3 D's will definitely cause some emotional hindrance*

Enough drama to have you disturbed and make your soul feel absence
Yet, some of those crises are just an example of one's crude flagrance
The other personalities involved may have you seeking vengeance
Deep down in your heart this tragedy should only be transience...

Because I have always trusted that patience and temperance resonate in what you advise

I continually attempt to take past, present and future transgressions in stride

Your philosophies provide me with a fresh breath of air

Making it a waste of time to wallow in regret or despair

I have become more limber and willing to remove my mask

Yet I will always only do it for those deserving and not everyone that asks

Not all are worthy of seeing the real me

Discretion, decorum and decency are the new 3 D's of my decree

As I am blessed to be growing not just older but wiser too

I figured out there is always a lesson from whatever one may go through...

Listen to your Own Self

He told me he loved me so many times…

Causing a sense of security that I craved – the fault was mine.

If I'd have only paid attention to his actions...

I would not be involved in this unsavory faction.

With a cornucopia of women calling MY phone…

One even had the audacity to be on MY cell asking was he "at home".

She asked so sweet and innocently I could not find the bile to raise MY voice.

I just said no and hung up…baffled at why denial was MY choice…

Because he told me he loved me so many times…

Being alone was my fear – so – yeah the fault is all mine.

On another day I noticed a change in MY physical make up…

An unusual texture and aroma that made me wonder what was up.

When I got the result I was relieved it was only bacterial…

Even this did not make me confront him – convinced myself I was just wearing the wrong materials.

He told me he loved me so many times…

Low self – esteem steering me into misleading MY OWN mind.

I was so determined to be with this so called man…

I ignored all warnings and delayed all plans.

MY mama, sister, brother and even MY friends…

Could not convince me that he was not for me and on him I could not depend.

He would borrow MY car while I was at work…

Never picked me up on time – while I paced out front – going berserk.

The tank would be on empty and the interior reeked of smoke…

While he laughed - as I complained - as if I were a joke.

And when we'd get home – behind that closed door…

He would strip me of all defenses and make me scream for more.

Afterward – I'd lie on MY side listening as he moved about MY home…

In the kitchen, the laundry room rambling as if MY things were his own.

I would ignore the feeling deep down that something was amiss…

And try to block out MY conscious asking…why do you tolerate this?

Because he told me he loved me so many times…

Self-worth was a concept that MY being could not even define.

The final straw was the birth of a child…

Not from MY womb but from one down the road a couple of miles.

I believed all his lies and claims that this child was not his…

Even stayed thru the paternity result - shared in the anxiety of this special quiz.

He expected me to still be the same…

To give myself over without any shame.

Because he told me he loved me so many times…

Eventually the truth is so apparent – there is no other disguise.

As I watched him verbally abuse and mistreat this woman who had just bore his seed…

A yearning to separate myself began to take heed.

By separate I mean I woke up and began to pay attention to MY intuition…

Bringing self-worth and esteem to fruition on every condition.

This boy pretending to be a man was no longer welcomed within MY realm…

MY mind, heart, and spirit had become so overwhelmed.

Filled to the brim with distaste when I would see his face…

He would stop by every now and again, all humble and disgraced.

Begging to stay the night, take me out or just be in my presence…

His touch would bring butterflies inside me of a queer essence.

Not the twinge of arousal but these stinging pricks of coldness …

With blinders removed all that remained of him was his ugliness and boldness.

Annoyance with myself that it had taken me so long to see…

Puzzled at why I had allowed this poor excuse to confuse me.

Because he told me he loved me so many times…

Relieved that listening to MY own self is truly sublime.

Name Calling….

Arrogant I was once called – I disagree as this reflects the strong stability of me…

Why? - Because I walk with my head held high and possess a lot of dignity…

The pessimistic attitude is only how you perceive it to be.

How do we subdue this anger?

Name calling – As if I was a stranger.

Greedy someone proclaimed - Greedy, I am not – what's wrong with being happy….

Get what you want and live life how it should be.

I can't help that they stare and my sexiness is all they see…

How do we subdue this anger?

Name calling – As if I was a stranger.

Spoiled I heard many times before– there's nothing wrong with being satisfied…

Understand there's nothing about me that can be modified…

Take me as I am since I can't be simplified.

How do we subdue this anger?

Name calling – As if I was a stranger.

Wicked some may claim –nothing about me desperately demands fame…

No explanation about my personality should I have to name…

The evil you portray must be a senseless game.

How do we subdue this anger?

Name calling – As if I was a stranger.

Mean was once spoken – proclaim the lack of consideration…

Untrue, as I constantly inspire mental concentration…

I long for your honesty to exceed my expectation.

How do we subdue this anger?

Name calling – As if I was a stranger.

Selfish someone stated a while ago…

Not true – maybe it's a strong reflection of my ego…

Self-centered, egotistic I am not! I oppose & say no.

How do we subdue this anger?

Name calling – As if I was a stranger.

Liar some may profess…

Games played often - I must confess…

Words you mumble – why do you digress.

How do we subdue this anger?

Name calling – As if I was a stranger.

The ATES that ACHE

It's hard to concentrate...when resting or working I contemplate... nothing is profound as this introspection as of late...unable to muster the energy to debate - surrounded by situations that frustrate... sighing, confused, resisting the urge to debilitate...oh Lord lift my spirit from this state...this feeling sitting on my heart is the heaviest weight…

Maybe to relieve this aggravation I just need to vacate…vanish into thin air where no one will see my face until my birth date…then again – that would be silly and immature in turn making many irate…just feel more often than not I am floating around out here all alone and it makes me desperate to escape – growing queasy at no ones ability to understand me or translate…to relate – let me attempt to restate…

The images and situations tugging at my heart leading to this fate…here goes – if interested notate…or perhaps there is advice you can donate, either of which would be great… the lackadaisical and disheartened condition of our society is what makes me fixate…it's as if we are not humans but spores of mold seeking water to hydrate…so that we can infect and congregate to execrate….

When an individual is enlightened most do not attempt to relate…but begin a campaign of envy promoting a theme of hate…this leads to only negative things and without a doubt increases the death rate…this fact should make awareness in our society inflate… sadly it does not even titillate…when observed the channel is simply switched as some new reality show is coming on at eight…

Up Tow

I don't think you realize how deep I go nor how long my emotions have existed in this up tow…this mixture, this delusion, confusion…searching, imagining, praying all would eventually meet find some – some sort of fusion…something…someone to understand, to empathize with all the muck, the ugliness I have witnessed, been a victim of, and yes even participated in…but it all depends…daylight again…eventually…one day hopefully you will be able to comprehend…my friend…that this here…this routine we deal with called life is beating me down, and most days I struggle with trying not to let it win…

I crave a relationship that so many I love and cherish I know would refuse to accept…and it's cool with me because on this level, this deep intimacy that would quench my thirst all it would need to grow is respect…see…**I don't think you realize how deep I go nor how long my emotions have existed in this up tow**…nah, you don't even know…this craziness, this blindness, mindlessness…this desperation, starvation, contemplation, building this dream up in my imagination…things I have said…done…at the end of the day there is only one who can bring that calm…

Doing so much running around that by the end of days most times I am drawn, moody, and listless…my mind exhausted but still going a mile a minute thinking what is this…wondering what happened…why what I want is not here or on its way, every night…my domicile…ours, the place we both stay…**I don't think you realize how deep I go nor how long my emotions have existed in this up tow**…this desire, this fire, needing your presence to inspire…ME…you must be blind if you cannot see…nah you don't even know…confused, bewildered, wondering where did your emotional compass go…OH, I KNOW…

Oh yeah, I know…you traded it in for a newer more efficient tool…and added that switch you can turn on and off that makes you instantly go cold…we used to be so similar…just alike at our core levels but as of late all of that is put on hold…oh no, **I don't think you realize how deep I go nor how long my emotions have existed in this up tow**…nah you cannot know…I am sure a glimpse into my heart, mind, or spirit would frighten you so…you…you the one who always has the right thing to say…a master at manipulating, contemplating, forever cautious always knowing the correct pawn to play…but like a sucker I sit here telling myself that you are just in a way…a way that will pass…undoubtedly because you know that even if not me someone or something will bring you to your knees, penetrating your mask…

It should make your heart skip a beat how deep I go and how long my emotions have been in this up tow…because it's you, from that day I first laid eyes on your face that let me know…this here my friend goes deeper, further than you will ever have the courage to show…**nah you have no idea how deep I go and how long my emotions have existed in this up tow**…

SPIRIT

Advice - A Narrative

"What is the best way to get over a man you've been involved with for years?" asked Renee as she ran a finger over her apple green iPod, reviewing songs she had recently downloaded.

"Hmm...Good question. Do you really want to know or are you just asking?" replied Yvonne as she closely inspected the index nail she was vigorously filing into a perfect square.

"Why you always doing that...answering a question with a question?", "That's rude!", "Answer me straightout youngin!" Renee snapped playfully, as she was only one year older than Yvonne.

"Okay, fine!! The only reason I asked is to be sure this is what you want to do...Are you ready to do this FOR REAL this time?" Yvonne replied.

"I don't know..." Renee said. "I feel so unsure about where I will end up if I leave.", "I tell myself to get out while there are no children involved, that this is the time to move on, I even pray about it but it's like my heart still hesitates. He knows all of the things to say to press my buttons - whenever I mention that I am unhappy with something he does, he flips it - you know what I'm saying ...flips the script so I will feel like I am in the wrong. We finally discussed what happened Friday about that money and you know what he said?"

"I know this is going to be real hard, but I am willing to help you get through this..." "Remember he is not who made you so, let that fear go... I know easier said than done...Yes, it will be extremely worse if you have a child...I was once told that misery loves company...Of course, he knows what to do, so will the next REAL MAN...The difference will be, he will love you and not push buttons to make you unhappy...Yea, all boys knows how to flip flop...I mean I can go on and on about the excuses boys say to make you want to stay, but I won't...So, what was the outcome with the money situation... I can probably guess how it went."

"He said..."You are so cold. I never would have done that to you. If you were going to work and I was staying home - boom no problem, here is my debit card - especially if I had just gotten paid. Damn, why don't you trust me? You act like I am going to go and charge like 200 bones on your card or something...damn.", For a second - I actually felt guilty Yvonne, like I needed to check myself, then it clicked in my head...he's just talkin'. He even played the family card, girl! "You really are beginning to act like your Mom..." relayed Renee as she shook her head, grinning while mimicking Breon's voice in high whiney tone." I just looked at him and said - whatever..."

"Wow!!!"..."He is really using the guilt card...Look Renee, this is his way to manipulate you by making you second guess yourself...Yea, he is saying anything he can to make you have a change of heart...Don't that fool know that families are off limits," Yvonne said as she was shaking her head no. "Girl, he must have lost his mind, I am speechless...I want to slap him."

"Disrespectful is the name of the game he plays...he is always stepping over lines that just should not be crossed, he honestly feels like I owe him an apology about not giving him my debit card. How did I let this happen to myself, this is what kindness gets you. Anyway...spill - what does a Sista have to do to break away from this mess...stop holding out and tell me."

"Okay, you asked for it... First, you need to STOP feeling so guilty about what you do for him... He is a grown man - supposedly...Once you stop feeling sorry for him you can focus on a time-frame that you want to be gone. There - is that good enough for you?"

Renee tilted her head and stared at her friend smiling, thinking to herself - DUH, knowing Yvonne she knew to keep quiet and listen. Yvonne could be a hot head but was smarter than anyone she'd met and was a truly generous soul, so she knew if she paid close enough attention she'd get the help she needed. "Okay...what's second?"

"Renee, take my hand...Listen, you are a strong, intelligent, Black woman, so don't be afraid to leave".... "I know leaving someone you love can be hard... So, I will stay calm and have patience with you"...Yvonne said softly..."The next thing to do is find you a place"..."Wait -wait, wait... have you been saving money as we discussed?"

"Saving money?"...Renee sighed and hesitated. "No...But...there are lots of specials right now. I did register with that service that helps people find places - someone already called and e-mailed me. I am sure I can get in a spot soon. Even if I have to eat oodles of noodles for a while...shoot I could stand to skip a couple of meals anyway. Everyone in my immediate family knows the situation so if any emergency happens all I have to do is open my mouth...why you doing that? Why you looking at me like that? Why do I have to meet all your little bullet points before you just tell me what I need to do? The whole reason I came to you is I am too emotional about it. When I think on it all these other issues get in the way. Be your practical self and give me the tools I need to make this happen." Renee pleaded…although she sounded frustrated she was doing as she always did…cling to anger to prevent her vulnerability from showing.

"See you want help but, you don't want to listen…Yvonne said, firmly, shaking her head in disbelief." Yes, there may be a lot of specials…BUT, the purpose of saving the money was so you would have a comfort zone…Fine!! Skipping meals, I hope this is one of your jokes again…I am looking at you like this because…How do you want me to look at you when you saying this? Okay, you right let me just tell you what to do…Will that make you happy?" Start slowly packing your things and possibly moving the stuff that is least noticeable out of the apartment"…After you found the place and have the date set you'll just need to pick a day and move all of your stuff at once while he is gone"…No, before you even say it…There is no more waiting for him to get this or buy that"…Remember he is the same one that left you with nothing"…"I am not saying an eye for an eye, but you need to put yourself first and do what Renee needs to in order to survive"...GOT IT!!" Yvonne yelled.

Renee looked at Yvonne...really looked at her - what she saw in her eyes made it impossible for her to get upset that she had yelled. She knew that everything Yvonne said was truth that could no longer be denied or avoided..., "I got it...she said as she reached out and hugged her friend." Thank you..."

At Any Cost

    Your attempt to intimidate -
debilitates – irritates,
aggravates – and just overall
frustrates

    Debilitation originating
from the frustration of the
lack of communication in
getting things straight...

Convinced you just don't have what it takes

To maturely show a decent character and openly disseminate...

Digression is a constant choice to avoid making another mistake

As reaching an understanding in any confabulation is no longer an objective desired to undertake...

Your intimidation attempts are downright comical

As your confidence is flimsy – an illusion, not actual, untactful and in no way factual...

The weakness and fear in your eyes is so heartfelt it is palpable

So tangible it leads you as if you are its toy thing to handle...

As you are so recalcitrant – preoccupied that imaginary eyes are watching – waiting on you to stumble...

So wrapped in your own misery you are blind to the human requisite to be humble

Butterflies

Today was the day that my stomach begin to burn

It was too late to turn around or show any signs of concern

My body is ready to go, but my heart wants to stay

Thinking to myself – "If only my plane had a day delay"

Then these butterflies might go away

So - I could focus on what I want to say

I knew this day was coming so I don't understand why

This sensation I am having deep down inside - is a ailment that I cannot deny

I dreamed about this day for the last two nights

I woke up to the sound of the alarm and morning daylight

I am looking good and feeling fine - so off to the airport I go

Sitting tight, ready for my flight... Soon the plane would be up in the wind flow

Can't U See

Do you see what I see?

When you look do you truly observe the inner me?

Or do you only have a narrow view...

Unfocused and unclear as to what we are going thru...

Our time together has not been spent on a crystal stair...

Regardless of where we lay our heads I will always care

Happiness and peace must soon arrive at our door...

Or we shall sink fast with no hope of making it to shore

Holding tight to our dream of making it together

Shunning all haters and lasting thru any kind of weather

In this I am still attempting to believe...

Wholeness, wealth and progressiveness – all this we can achieve…

Domestic Violence

<u>HE</u>

Taking a long drag on a cig

He threw his head back and looked at the sky – choking back tears at what he'd did…

Now he knew things had gotten really bad

Arguments and fighting blocked out all images of what they'd had…

It used to be so easy to just kiss and make up

He sighed – looking down and tried to remember when they're relationship became so corrupt…

SHE

Cradling the phone in her hand debating if she should dial

Eye stinging, lip swollen- heart pounding as if she'd run a mile…

So angry and confused that she could not think

Recalling past disagreements – shaking her head yes – she had taken him to the brink

Before he had never struck her in the face

But this time she could not hide her disgrace…

Everyone who caught a glimpse would definitely know

Her relationship was abusive - not that she stayed due to fear of where to go

HE

Man I hope she forgives me and lets me back in…

Maybe if I explained when she talks to me like that – it's my manhood I must defend

Nah, that won't work – I've used that excuse so many times

I smacked her in the face – everyone will know – an unforgivable crime...

She might actually call the cops because she is so into projecting the right image

I should probably go spend the night at a friend's – maybe play some cribbage

Empathy

Taking deep breathes -holding on to words

that are so hard to express...

Tears of sadness not seeing your smile another day

is hard to digest.

The lasting impression you had on people that crossed your path was so profound...

Not knowing how to pick up the pieces - Lost in a maze - sort of a daze looking around.

Trying to realize the last time was the final one - I'd laugh with you...

Heaven was overdue for another angel... now you're gone –

I know this is true.

I can see through your mask....

When we are unsure what to do we tend to hide behind a facade

Even if we know what we are doing is portraying a fraud

Not realizing that the barricade we utilize is not what is within

The sooner you recognize – we are different – the friendships can begin

I can see through your mask you are reaching out for relief - I want to help with your battle and

eliminate all of the grief…

I know there maybe pain that you do not want others to discover

So, you conceal yourself under a mask hoping no one will uncover

The aches, agony, aggravation, and heartbreak you have experienced in your life

All these tribulations has put a shield over your heart to protect you from more strife

I can see through your mask you are reaching out for relief - I want to help with your battle and

eliminate all of the grief…

When I first met you my mind use to say, "with all the drama why bother"

I didn't know the attitude may have come when you lost your father

Once I talked with you about the past my eyes begin to shed a tear

Then I read your poetry you seemed the total opposite of how you appear

I can see through your mask you are reaching out for relief - I want to help with your battle and

eliminate all of the grief…

I stay true no matter what others perceive me out to be

If you know me then you will say – she is constantly true to me

A genuine friend that is honest, loyal, reliable and always keeps it real

Then soon the process for your heart, body and soul commence to heal

I can see through your mask you are reaching out for relief - I want to help with your battle and

eliminate all of the grief...

After listening to you for a while I realized you just want to be understood

What you are feeling could be stemming from an incident that happened during your childhood

No one knows the emotion we hold on to that brings us alive

I just wish that we can show the authentic you and not all this jive

Inspired by Friendship, Love, and Concern

It is imperative in life to have the ability to change your degree…

What I am speaking of is simple – requires no loan or scholarship – it is totally free…

To earn this degree only switch channels in your heart, spirit and mind…

Similar to a tuning dial in your soul, the button is easy to find…

Change the way you process thoughts, images, and feelings…

Perfecting this is the meaning of happiness and fosters healing…

Lately, the trend in our society is to contemplate a microwaveable way to be "successful" – how to come up in a hurry…

This trend, the current economy, and overall atmosphere in our world make many fearful – full of dread and worry…

Be assured success is not determined by the dollars you make; it is truly measured by how you overcome struggle, destruction, fear and all the things to follow in it's wake…

Be still my friends – resilient in your journey on being close to our heavenly father…

Only observe intelligently these worldly issues and persist in your prayers; securing the hope - these matters will not always bother…

Lessons and Blessings

Blushing all day as seeing him again…

Makes memories flood my mind – the most prevalent is reminiscent of how his touch felt upon my skin…

His complexion and facial expressions are twirling around as well…

With the meeting of our eyes we each behaved as if under some spell…

He was athletic and loved to play sports…you know the type of brother who sought out competition of any sort…

But lessons – come in all kinds of dressings – pay attention or you may miss your blessings…

He was wrapped around my finger and I his…

The way we made each other's blood pump – see this was our first encounter confirming we were no longer kids…

When standing close to me – he never lied and was quick to make any confession…

As the slightest touch from me could cause him to get an erection…

He was easy to arouse as we were so young – I can still feel the goose bumps he caused with that tongue…

Of his…all over me – passionately – instantaneously insistent we make this a commitment – permanently, undoubtedly and completely…

But lessons – come in all kinds of dressings – pay attention or you may miss your blessings…

I will attempt to digress – yes cannot help but confess I was taken aback – dare I say even shook…

Well I guess this is what happens now days when you join social networks like face book…

Hesitant to admit the havoc he caused when he walked out of my life –

More so even as with the click of my mouse – yep – there is a picture of him and his common law wife…

But lessons – come in all kinds of dressings – pay attention or you may miss your blessings…

She is pretty – truthfully I am not jealous, envious or upset…

The two of them make a wonderful couple I bet…

Perhaps if we had not been broken I would not be who I am today…

With all kinds of obstacles steadily still standing in my way…

But lessons – come in all kinds of dressings – pay attention or you may miss your blessings…

Seeing his face brought in a hovering - this nagging sensation in my heart…

That back then I believed losing him would tear me apart –

All the nights he held and kissed me so sure I would be his match...

Never once thinking another could distract...

You see in life everyone that speaks is not always telling you the truth...

This realization can be painful but is something we all must go thru...

My Heart Don't Pump No Slushy (even though it may seem so)

It does not even bother me when folk don't understand...

I am fronting – it stings – but I have to keep moving... just rationalize that they just were not part of the PLAN...

Not part of the scenario that is my life

Don't possess what is necessary and don't have a particular device

An instrument or dare I say mechanism to appreciate who I may be...

Just a woman out here adjusting, maneuvering and searching for the most comfortable degree

The right spot where I don't feel too hot or too cold

Not fazed and stressed by whatever or whoever may be buying or being sold...

It does not even bother me when folk don't understand...

I am fronting – it stings – but I have to keep moving... just rationalize that they just were not part of the PLAN...

In dreams the world is perfect and no one ever disagrees

I am romantic yet a realist so I appreciate facing realities

The cold hard truth is everybody is not meant to be the closest of friends

You know that rock – always solid and strong and on one can always depend…

I admit I get weak when burdens become too much to bear

Will flee and withdraw as I have only one heart and no spare…

It does not even bother me when folk don't understand…

I am fronting – it stings – but I have to keep moving… just rationalize that they just were not part of the PLAN…

But once I have taken time to rationalize and make sense of the overflow of my senses

This is when the best part of my being commences

I heard tell in a song that has one of the most resounding of melodies

To get to the sweetest nectar of forgiveness and happiness each of us has to find peace with our own complexities…

Self-acceptance brings a wholeness within that is one of the most rewarding in life's journey

Making respecting who I am and others simple and outstandingly discerning…

It does not even bother me when folk don't understand…

I am fronting – it stings – but I have to keep moving… just rationalize that they just were not part of the PLAN…

Today's Flights Require Distraction

Do what you want to do

Regardless of that extra others may attempt to put you thru...

If an embrace brings on that certain chemistry

Don't second guess yourself and get all feisty...

If a touch causes those tickly, tingly, bubbles to form in your belly

Relax and go with it instead of getting all scary...

Do what you want to do

Regardless of that extra others may attempt to put you thru...

If you look in those bronze eyes and feel any trace of a chill

Hang loose, smile and convince him his presence alone is a thrill...

Now I know these are things a socialite such as you already knows

Just to reassure either choice is no reason to forgo

Do what you want to do

Regardless of that extra others may attempt to put you thru...

Sympathy

In the light of today and the promise of dawn tomorrow...

Continue to look heavenward to chase away those sorrows.

Taking as much time as you need to heal...

Trusting that you are not alone in the way that you feel...

This difficulty you are suffering is only temporary.

Soon your sadness will pass and joy will not seem so contrary...

Just a note to let you know my thoughts are with you and inner strength for you is what I pray.

Although I cannot see you, I know
you become stronger day by day...

Think Before You Speak

Was, is and always will be a liar...

The onset of this realization can distinguish all traces of desire

In the bedroom, the kitchen, the car or any space that is occupied at the same time

Every answer to any question has to be weighed for accuracy as if on maritime

Let me break it down as to why I say all this

Believing lies can lead you down wrong paths as all sense of direction goes amiss

Was, is and always will be a liar...

The onset of this realization can distinguish all traces of desire

Had to check myself to be sure it was not just me

Verified that some individuals treat everyone with this type of revelry

It's as if lying is part of their physical make up

Telling the truth about the smallest thing causes some sort of disrupt

Was, is and always will be a liar...

The onset of this realization can distinguish all traces of desire

To their system and wellbeing – it becomes their most practiced habit

Like a cigarette or drink it's their crutch and security blanket

People lie to others for all types of reasons...

To throw them off of what is factual – sometimes because they take joy in deceiving

Was, is and always will be a liar...

The onset of this realization can distinguish all traces of desire

Believe me when I say and old souls will let you know…

Lie, steal, kill is the only way this negative progression goes

If you realize this practice is one in which you often partake

I beg you stop now before it's too late…

Too Much of Anything Isn't Good for You

Addiction originates from within

Usually when one is in a weakened state, well that is the trend…

There are hosts of reasons one may experience this affliction

Any excuse one can think of – even heredity – has been used to explain this condition…

Now it's tradition to kick back – to lay troubles down every now and then

But if this is done daily – no matter the substance – this is where the trouble begins…

The substance becomes everything

Reducing some of the greatest jewels to mere puppets on a string…

Rushing thru any task to get back
to that crutch – the master

Never minding who notices quality
of life has become a disaster...

Why Some Black Women Mean Mug...

She tends to frown...

No matter who's around due to her sensitivity and more often than not the state of the world makes her feel down...

She is usually pondering on what someone said or something she's seen...her seriousness comes naturally but gives the impression that she is mean...

She lives inside her head – yes her imagination runs deep...

Can be over cautious and observe with eagle eyes her surroundings when walking down streets...

The reason she is this way is simple – bright ones catch it every time...

She is soft-hearted and slow to recover – so she is convinced she must stay on the grind...

The grind of keeping it moving – hopping from object, to subject, to task...

Sure to avoid eye contact for fear of revealing her masks...

Underneath which she is really nurturing, loving, and sweet...

Believing many will jump on that opening – wolves in sheep's clothing – you know discreet...

Will she ever be safe in this wilderness called life...?

Doubts cloud her mind – fear also but never strife...

Inside – she sees sunlight on the horizon...

Hope, promise, and happiness by the dozen...

Enough to go around for everyone regardless of sex, class, or even race...

Where we all can be free to show our real face...

PROFOU ND

IMAGERY

After work

Standing at my bureau – removing
jewelry and such

Behind me I feel a presence – then
upon my waist a touch

You pull me closer – solidifying our embrace

I wonder somewhere far within my mind – if you can feel my heartbeat – it has begun to race

You must as you lean in to gently place a kiss upon my ear

This is what I've needed all day – I bite my lip to fight back a joyful tear

As I turn in your arms and hungrily kiss your lips

This familiar taste – the sweetest nectar – my favorite thing to sip…

Cupcakes can be Hazardous to One's Health

When you walk by you look as delectable as a cupcake

I want to reach out and perform a taste test but do not for decorum's sake...

It is unfair that muscle on bone should possibly be so tempting

So many eyes lingering on you like a tigress eyeing her next killing...

The only reason I haven't stepped to you is ... I just don't know what to say

You cause me to get all tongue tied, confused convinced words will just get in the way...

Your sex appeal makes me yearn for the days of acting with no cause or reason

When things were less risky and it was safe to get physical – the only concern being - pleasing...

But in these days and times when your sexiness has happened across my path

I must be responsible and ponder if getting to the get down will lead to an unhealthy aftermath...

Rejection has never even entered into my consciousness

I can feel, no smell, yes even taste your willingness to get with this...

But I will just continue to admire the way you glide as if well-oiled from afar

Reluctant to let this inclination slide and become only a memoir

Maturity and wisdom have granted me much needed self-control

Seems like only minutes have passed but it has been years since I participated in any meaningless bedrolls...

I will settle for only fantasying about having you behind a closed door

Each of us being greedy remaining insatiably gluttonous and taking more...

When you walk by you look as delectable as a cupcake

I want to reach out and perform a taste test but will not for decorum's sake...

Dropped From Heaven

I would have taken you however you had come

In whatever dress, body type or race as you really show a special magnetism

You look pass all the petty, silly, meddling things I do just to get my way

Make me feel special, beautiful, smart and sexy each and every day…

I give praise to the most high for making you the way you are

Understanding, strong, kind, and upon one of the best physically to gaze by far…

Never pretentious or fake because you are convinced there is no such thing as half way crooks

All your lessons learned thru experience and some from movies and books…

This concoction that is you is breathtakingly the truth

That down home southern goodness – yes the best brew.

Fruity Fantasies

If I were a peach would you take a bite of me?

Slurping, gulping and swallowing as if tasting the sweetest daiquiri...

Or as I gleam in the sunlight like the ripest strawberry.

Red yet pink when you partake making me beg for mercy....

Or luscious yet hairy like a scrumptious kiwi.

Sucking with all your strength – forcing me to open and give my all to you freely...

Or firm and subtle like those pineapples you love.

That hole in the center fitting the length of you so snug...

Trembling as your tongue, hands, and fingers glide down my body sensuously...

Entering, fingering, and eating until each of us are satisfied completely.

Hoping this message reaches and clearly commutes...

Just wondering what you'd do if I were one of your favorite pieces of fruit.

Grown Folk Passion

He is grasping me from behind kissing the backsides of me with abandon...

Before I can think of a reasonable protest – an excuse why this should not happen.

He is on his knees in front of me, his tongue seeking my clitoris to dampen…

It must be the fresh air making me light headed, every nerve ending tingly and sensitive to the touch.

He is holding my thighs in his huge hands spreading, licking, each of us moaning as upon his head I clutch…

Looking down titillates making me so hot, my mind shouts to just go with it and don't deny.

His tongue, fingers, and feel of his lips on my lower lips – taking only seconds before I feel my bones liquefy…

He catches me, and lifts me before allowing me to slip to the floor.

Cradling and caressing me – he whispers, "Baby, please let me do more"…

So insistent is his stare as I dizzily look into his eyes.

It's clear this is not a question it's a request that cannot be denied…

Choked up I pull his head to mine for a deep kiss.

With every smack and suckle urging him to get at this…

So that nothing is misunderstood I say seductively, "Get at me".

Pulsating and wet, tonguing his sexy mouth, my hand moving up and down the center of him as my silent plea…

Inside my belly lurches forth a need - an overwhelming desire.

Only one thing can distinguish this inferno and totally stamp out this fire...

Stiffness stands proud and strong at the end of his pelvis.

It is my turn to be on my knees – oh how I enjoy this...

Could it be possibly more pleasurable for me to feel him as I take him into my mouth?

Hard, powerful and male yet I am in complete control without a doubt...

With each lick, suckle, and yes the slightest maneuver.

Makes him grunt, shudder and totally surrender...

Forgetting my needs - to his I totally submit.

Stroking with my tongue and lips until he emits...

What seems like ounces of what makes him a man deep into my throat.

Savoring the taste and feel I eagerly swallow every gulp...

Muse

My talent comes from deep within

If things are not right – my energy just does not blend

Grateful to have found a muse

A powerful force to provide that extra boost

Someone who stirs me up

Honest, easily laughs and not corrupt

A banging personality – the coolest and does not even know

Possessing a glow as natural to them as breathing to show

A light so bright it can be blinding as if looking into the sun

Able to show integrity - when necessary aggression to be sure things get done

A chemistry exist between us

Done the research each born on cusps

A mixture of water and air

Each forgiving but never forget any source of despair

Toward the middle experienced a situation similar to demise

Trusting everything is for a reason reached a compromise

One too open the other moves in slow motion to reveal

A combination with practice soon to show high appeal…

Rationale within the Un-rational...the Sensual and Sexual

I've got a boyfriend – and a girlfriend too...

Who comes over at night depends on how I want to be held and what I am going thru.

This doesn't mean I am greedy, needy, shady, or a freak...

Perhaps just honest and a pleasure seeker - behind that closed door a beast.

Sure I could play by the "rules" – let society, friends, and family dictate or define me.

But even that would not diminish my attraction to he or she...

My girl is a thinker, gentle, and sweet almost like a best friend...

My man is thoughtful, protective, and strong – on him I can depend.

I know many may be thinking – I bet they have threesomes and those crazy parties – the

whole nine...

But believe me when I tell you – when I am with either of them – they are selfish with my time.

Satisfied but Still Hungry

Exactly 13 days passed before you delivered on your love declaration

Your tendency to move in slow-motion is more than likely the explanation...

When you finally got around to it - I was about to burst at the seams

So wet with anticipation...yet trying to play it cool - to avoid being demeaned...

Just sidestepping the embarrassment that rushes forth after we have had one of our sessions

My moans, screams and orgasms are evidence enough so there is no need for a written confession...

You brought out every inch of my passion with those long deep strokes

I anxiously await the next evening for all your attention upon me you devote...

Sexual Orientation

This subject is tricky

As each person has an opinion and option – what is right or wrong gets sticky...

What variation of this activity an individual prefers is their choice.

Trouble occurs when someone tries to muffle another's voice...

To persuade, convince, or pressure what someone should be.

Is one of the many detriments in our society...

Shadows in Smoke

They are coming. They will be here in hours...only hours! These thoughts swirled in Sharee's mind as she nervously paced in her living room. Why did I even agree to this – I am so stupid! Throwing her hands in the air, she wearily plops down on her couch reaching for her cigarettes, she lights one and takes a long drag. Glancing to her left at the T.V. she was oblivious to the images on the screen... the images that were playing out in her mind were more vivid – only in black and white.

"I have been waiting a long time to have you and now I am here for what has always been mine", Mike said with a smirk. Shukri did not resist his embrace and kiss...she knew her Aunt would not be home for hours and even though the man kissing her was her cousin – it was no big deal she rationalized, he was sexy and she had always wanted him besides technically they were only related through marriage. It wasn't until he pushed that final thrust into her that she remembered – he used to do this to me when I was little, memories rushed to her consciousness. His smell – he still smells the same. Looking into his eyes as they both heaved air into their lungs; she was disgusted, afraid and angry all at once. "Damn girl, I knew you had that good pussy.", "Let me get out of here before Mom gets back." Mike muttered as he got up looking for his pants.

Spontaneity

As you walk into our bedroom with an exhausted and contemplative look on your face at the day you've had...you glance over at me on our bed and our eyes meet. Seeing your expression makes me inquire, "What's wrong baby, everything alright?" you reply, "Yes, just tired". You begin to undress; removing your blouse and slacks...I walk over to stand behind you placing one hand on your waist and the other on your shoulder. I pull you close, holding you as I bend my head to kiss your shoulder, burrowing my nose into your neck, kissing and inhaling deeply taking in as much air as possible because I love the way you smell. You exhale and I can feel some of the tension leave your body. You relax and lean your head on my chest..., "I love you", I whisper..."I love you too", you reply. I turn your body in my arms and look into your eyes...I am always amazed at how beautiful you are and this time is no exception. Your eyes are the color of cinnamon...set in an exquisite face; its shape reminds me of a honey colored heart. As my eyes come to rest on your mouth I am consumed with the desire to kiss you…to taste and feel those lips of yours that I adore. As I bend my neck intent on doing just that you lean in and take my bottom lip into your mouth…sucking and licking its fullness. This causes my knees to go weak…making my clitoris tingle and sprinkle in reaction to your kiss. You are now embracing me tightly and passionately walking forward forcing me to walk backward until I feel the side of our bed on the backs of my legs. I sit on the bed as you bend at your waist ensuring we stay connected at our lips while pushing me back as you straddle my waist with your legs. You are on me and over me…breaking our kiss only to kiss and lick my cheeks and neck before reclaiming my lips again and again. I love the way you kiss…it is always perfect, a passionate variation of your lips and tongue...never too hard or too soft. Suddenly you stop and look into my eyes...as I stare up at you while you are shirtless and blushing - I cup your breast, running the pads of my thumbs across your nipples...you close your eyes and arch your back...with your head thrown back you say, "Baby...I missed you so much today."...I sit up, taking one of your cocoa nipples into my mouth...I say, "How much did you miss me?", "Mmmm...So much..." you whisper as I suck you...making your nipple pucker and harden...I suck...then lick...flickering your sensitive flesh with my tongue as you swell in my mouth. I release one nipple only to suck the other...leaving traces of my kisses all over your chest. I run my hand up to the back of your neck...for leverage as I move to sit up on my knees while you are still straddling me...you are now on your back and I am on and over you. I kiss down your tummy, rubbing your thighs that are open at their widest for me to lie in between. I slip your panties to the side with my index and middle finger...what I find at the center of you is a soft yet firm pond...so slick and intoxicating in the way that you feel on my fingers. As I caress you...moving my fingers in slow circles over your clitoris you moan, grabbing and pulling at my hair...I am so hypnotized by the feel of you I barely notice this...you become insistent forcing me to look at you, "What's wrong?", I ask...you respond, "Baby, let me shower...I just got off work." As I look at your well kissed mouth, hard nipples standing out still wet from my tongue, with legs spread just for me...I place my fingers covered with you in my mouth and whisper, "Mmmm...please...let me taste you...stop worrying - you're delicious", to prove this fact I place the fingers I just licked in your mouth...as you lick my fingers and taste yourself I use my other hand to push your panties from your hips...I replace my fingers with my lips...slowly lapping at your gorgeous mouth and ask you, "See how good you taste?", staring into my eyes you nod your head yes..."Say it Baby...say "I taste good"...say it", I plead...you take my bottom lip into your mouth once again and gently bite and suck it before whispering, "I taste good."...I look into your eyes...sure that your irises mirror my own in what we both want and need...I begin to kiss your neck, down the center of your chest, to your belly...and finally arrive at the apex of your thighs...I close your legs for a second to remove your panties - throwing them to the side of our bed. I lay on my stomach balancing my weight on my elbows while holding your thighs apart as I kiss first your left inner thigh and then your right. Licking and sucking your luscious thighs, reveling in the scent and feel of you I feel as if I am drowning in my senses - surrounded by your moans, the way you feel, look and taste...I am yours. I slowly begin to kiss and lick around the heart of you...while you run your fingers thru my hair...urging me - silently pleading for me to lick your clit...I decide I have waited long enough and hover above your clitoris...only for a second...purposely allowing you to feel my breath on this - the most sensitive part of your body...inhaling deeply to take in the scent of you, I love the way you smell...I close the inches between my mouth and your clit...latching on to your clit...flicking it left then right...you are so wet now...raining wet...as I gently dart my tongue across, over and under your clit - I reach up to grasp both your breasts in either hand...flicking your nipples with my thumbs in the same rhythm as I am flicking your clit with my tongue. You are now holding onto whatever you can get your hands on...my hair, my head, the bed...the sheets..."Baby, I love you so much...I am yours Baby...damn Baby...", this encourages the quickening of my tongue as I vigorously lap your clit..., I whisper between licks...,"I love you Baby...cum...For...me...please Baby...cum." "That's what you want...ahhh Baby...you want me to cum...!!!, you scream, "Baby...mmm," you moan and whimper. I continually lick, smack and suckle your clit in the same pattern quickly and decisively...lick, smack, suckle ... as you arch your back I immediately slow my pace as I know you are close...lick.....smack.....suckle..., "Baby....damnnnnn baby...damnnnnn Ba....by...mmmmm...ahhhh, yesssss Baby....!!!", lick....smack suckle....you are quiet now breathing heavily....I began to kiss up your belly and concentrate on suckling your nipple while you run your hands thru my hair....you place your hand under my chin urging me to look at you...our eyes meet...you say to me..."I love it when you are spontaneous Baby..."

Trippin'

I'm moody.

No matter how much I pray that will change – it's just me

Is this the way I am meant to be?

Even though that one word does not describe me completely...

It's complicated – the way I feel

Afraid of rejection – if you'll see what's real

I'm insecure.

When I let you know the real me – would you flip it?

Flip out – become malicious, crafty and set to manipulate...

In this day and age – this is more often than not most relationships fate

Just need a kind soul - someone who understands...

What I am going thru...

Yeah I be trippin' – I know...it's true.

I'm quiet.

Someone even described me as simple – this made me squint – then smile

Showing my one dimple – thinking to myself what you know about me could not fill a thimble....

Why I Write Poems

Seldom does one get an opportunity to experience emotions this deep

As if on a precipice looking down into pits so steep

Wide open and exposed with main orifices screaming warnings of being on half empty

Yet every syllable is replenishing - reassuring there is plenty

An abundance of verses twitching to be unbound

Thoughts, emotions, fantasies, and overall creativity that is profound...

Complexity yields to simplicity – extracting that home grown brilliance

Smoothly moving past life's lessons...bravely outspoken with conscience

Dedication

I'd like to thank so many for contributing to the creation of this work – those who encouraged and motivated me. Always reassuring me that the way I put words together is a gift that should not be squandered...that my thinking is profound and eloquent...thank you as without you – I'd have never known...

The Most High...thank you for using me as a vessel that is sensitive and alert – I am humbled and grateful each day.

Tot...My muse, critic, nemesis and sister from another mother...my friend who without - I could not have completed this...

My Mama*...I am so grateful to have passed through you.*

My Daddy*...eccentricity at its best – I miss you every day – thank you for always letting me know it is perfectly fine to be different.*

My Sisters*...two beautiful women – who always tell me the truth as seen thru their own eyes – no matter how much it may sting.*

My Brother *- the first person I ever knew – you taught me life is meant to be lived.*

Mae*...Thank you for always seeing the beauty and talent in me.*

To all my friends and associates who read one of my poems, essays, or short stories and gave an opinion. I appreciate it and am grateful to each who took the time to read my thoughts, including every individual reading this right now, thank you so much...

Made in the USA
Columbia, SC
21 March 2020